Sam McBratney

The FIRETAIL CAT

Illustrated by Scoular Anderson

MACDONALD YOUNG BOOKS

3 8015 01143 3376

This '
date
bro'
tele

If \
th(

—

—

—

—

2

First published in Great Britain in 1995
by Macdonald Young Books Ltd
Campus 400
Maylands Avenue
Hemel Hempstead
Herts HP2 7EZ

Typeset in 14/20pt New Century Schoolbook by Dalia Hartman
Printed and bound in Portugal by Ediçoes ASA

British Library Cataloguing in Publication Data available

ISBN: 0 7500 1597 7
ISBN: 0 7500 1598 5 (pb)

There really were "firetail" cats
on board sailing ships. In some
kinds of weather a cat's coat can
give off static electricity - this is
what makes a balloon cling to a
wall after you rub it on your sleeve.

The sailors of long ago had never
heard of static electricity. When they
saw a "firetail" cat on board, they
were nervous...

This is a story about a firetail cat.

CHAPTER ONE

When the pirate ship *Belinda* sailed into harbour, most people went to bed early. They knew what the pirates were like, you see. They knew there would be trouble for someone tonight.

Aboard the pirate ship *Belinda*, Captain Jethro Pegg wrote out his shopping list:

Gunpowder for my guns.
A tin of polish
Walnuts for King George
A cabin boy
A ship's cat

Then he climbed into a small dinghy and rowed into town with three other villainous pirates. Their names were Edmund Scurf, Twiggy Blackstaff and Tiny Jacks. King George, the parrot, sat on the captain's left shoulder.

The shopkeeper's hands shook with fright as he read Pegg's list.

"B..b..but sir," he said, "I don't sell cabin boys and I don't sell cats."

"Not much of a shop," snarled Scurf.

"Sharkbait!" screeched the parrot. (Although King George was a talking parrot, he only knew one word.)

The pirates marched along to the harbour inn.

"Landlord!" cried Pegg. "We'll have three jugs of your best ale - and bring us your cat."

The landlord arrived with a trayful of ale and an armful of cat. The cat was a graceful animal with proud, pointed ears and a pair of liquid eyes, one blue and one green. Above her sleek coat there curled a marvellous tail, and this tail flowed gently when she moved.

"This here cat's not mine, Captain," said the landlord. "Don't know where she came from. I've heard folks say that she's a *firetail* cat."

Tiny Jacks leaned over to whisper into Pegg's right ear. "They say firetails glow in the dark, Cap'n. Cats like them is never lucky on board ship."

"She's bad luck, all right," scowled Pegg, as he shoved the cat into a sack. "Bad luck if you happen to be a *rat*. Let's drink up and go. We still have to find us a cabin boy."

Their last little cabin boy had jumped overboard. The poor lad had been so miserable on board the *Belinda* that he'd tried to swim away to freedom.

CHAPTER TWO

Young William Trevithick lived in a steep little street near the water's edge. In the morning he cut wood for burning. In the afternoon he collected edible seaweed and now, in the evening, he was making clay pots.

William worked so hard because his mother and father needed the money. His father had a wooden leg after serving with Lord Nelson in the King's navy.

As William rolled out clay by the light of a candle, there came a knock at the door.

"Captain Jethro Pegg at your service, boy," said the person with the parrot on his shoulder.

"Anyone else at home?"

"My father is asleep, sir, and my mother is serving at the inn."

William didn't like the look of this lot. Something wriggled inside the sack they had with them. He tried to shut the door in their horrible faces, but Pegg's boot stopped it from closing.

"I am here to offer you a job as a cabin boy on board the good ship *Belinda*."

"I don't want to be a cabin boy," said William.

"Congratulations," said Pegg, "you've got the job. Stick 'im in the sack, Scurf, and let's be off."

Although William did his best to struggle there wasn't much he could do against the four of them. He couldn't even shout inside the sack because his voice was muffled.

Something warm and furry wriggled under him in the sack. He felt the pit-a-pat of a little creature's quick heartbeat. It seemed to be a cat. William Trevithick cuddled it gently, because he felt that it might be as lonely and as frightened as he was.

What sort of things does a cabin boy *do*, he wondered.

RULES

Obey the Captain at all times.
No pistols.
No spitting below deck.
One cup of water a day.
Show respect for King George.
Never mention the Captain's treasure.
Do not feed the ship's cat.

CHAPTER THREE

"You do *everything*!" roared Jethro Pegg at breakfast next morning. "Whatever we ask. Whatever has to be done! You'll soon get used to it, won't he, King George?"

King George accepted a walnut from his master's pocket and crushed it in his beak.

"Yes," Pegg went on, "you'll scrub the deck, fetch me rum, oil the guns. We'll keep you busy, never fear - you won't have time to get bored."

It was a calm, bright morning. Looking around him, William could see no hint of land at the fringe of the sparkling ocean.

"I don't really want to be a cabin boy," he said.

Pegg merely smiled as he rose from his breakfast of bread and treacle. He walked to a plank that hung out over the sea. This plank didn't lead anywhere. It stopped in mid-air.

"Would you like to go for a long walk on a short plank? Would you rather be *sharkbait* than a cabin boy?"

"No, sir."

"Then take this tin of polish and follow me. I am about to show you your most important job of all."

Pegg led William below deck. At the bottom of the steps there were two doors side by side, one labelled GUNPOWDER, NO CANDLES and the other with no writing on it at all.

They entered the unlabelled room, where Jethro Pegg licked his lips as he feasted his eyes on gold bars and silver goblets and jewels that flickered with the movement of the candle's flame.

"One day I'll be the richest man in England, boy! Start polishing. And mind your thieving fingers because I count this lot every day. Now get busy."

William polished Pegg's hoard of stolen treasure until his arms ached. After a time he noticed two points of light glittering in the darkness. At first he thought they must be jewels - then they moved closer.

They were *eyes*.

"Puss? Is that you?"

A spray of blue sparks suddenly shot out from the cat's tail so that for an instant he saw the whole animal standing there. This was one of the spookiest things he had ever seen.

"I've heard about cats like you," he managed to whisper. "You can do magic. You're a *firetail*."

The cat came closer, and William took it on his lap. "Well if you can do magic, you'd better get us off this ship," he said to it. "Or I have an awful feeling that we'll both end up as sharkbait."

CHAPTER FOUR

Four pirates, including the ship's cook, sat up on deck. Their Captain was down below counting his treasure and so they were relaxing in the warm sun while eating apples from a barrel.

"If we bashed him over the head, you know," said Twiggy Blackstaff, "we could have all that lovely treasure for ourselves."

"Aye, that we could," agreed Scurf.

"We could buy ourselves a whole desert island with money like that," added Tiny Jacks, and for some moments the pirates dreamed of a golden beach with palm trees and free bananas.

"Allo-allo," said the ship's cook, "do you see what's happening over there?"

He meant the firetail cat, who lay on her back as she pawed at a loose rope dangling from a sail. Round and round went the rope. Round and round.

Scurf jumped to his feet with a mad, wild look in his eye. "The rope! The cat is turning the rope!"

"What about it?" asked Blackstaff.

"Don't you see? That means she's stirring up the wind. There'll be a storm for sure."

"Your head's a pancake," said Cook. "The sea is like glass, there's not a breath of wind."

"He might be right," said Tiny Jacks as he nervously stroked his pigtail. "I've heard stories about firetail cats that would make your hair curl."

"I'm telling you, I know about these things," cried Scurf. "A mate of mine had a firetail on his ship and they never had peace until they threw it overboard."

"Waste of good meat," said Cook. "Anyway, we'd better get busy before his lordship has finished counting his treasure."

The pirates threw their apple cores at the cabin boy and went below.

William Trevithick had been painting the deck with a horrible smelly tar, and he had heard every word those pirates said.

"Psst! You, Firetail! Did you hear all that? You'd better watch out. Scurf doesn't like you and Cook says you'd make a nice stew. If I was you I'd catch a few rats and keep them happy."

He didn't expect an answer, of course. The cat simply stared at him. Looking into those eyes, one blue and one green, William felt as though he were seeing through to a different world.

The cat stretched her long body lazily, then carried her floating tail to the steps that led below deck. And there she stood, gazing back at William.

"What is it?"

Did she want him to follow her? A rush of air swept in from the sea and the huge mainsail suddenly snapped full of wind, then went limp again. And still the cat waited for him. Did she know something?

Best to follow her, thought William. And she led him down narrow passages into the depths of the ship.

Soon the beams began to creak and the ship began to sway. Foaming waves crashed on the deck of the good ship *Belinda*, and the air was filled with salty spray and driven rain.

"To your posts, do you hear there!" bellowed Pegg above the storm. "Tie everything down. And lower the blasted *sails* or we're sharkbait, you bunch of gutless wonders!"

A barrel of apples rumbled across the deck, carrying Tiny Jacks overboard with it. The wind blew a pirate off the rigging as a wave washed two more over the starboard bow, and that was the end of them.

Far below William Trevithick lay curled up in a corner with the firetail cat, and all the while the great tall ship swayed and dipped and heaved in the heights and hollows of the raging sea.

CHAPTER FIVE

The damage was terrible. Seven pirates had been washed overboard by the storm - or maybe it was eight or nine, Jethro Pegg didn't much care. He had more important things to worry about. The sail hung in tatters. The main mast was down. Cannon balls rolled about the deck like giant marbles. And he'd lost his beloved King George in the storm.

"That foul cat did this to us, Cap'n," said Scurf. "Strike me pink if it didn't conjure up a gale out of a clear sky!"

Pegg picked up a cannon ball. His one good eye became a narrow slit of wickedness.

"Fetch me the brute. We'll sink it like a blasted stone. She'll cause no more trouble when she's at the bottom of the deep blue sea."

Joyfully, Twiggy Blackstaff and the Cook set off to hunt for the firetail cat. They spotted her in the doorway of the kitchen. She darted into the kitchen when she saw them coming.

"Got her now!" said Cook. "There's no way out of there."

They rushed into the kitchen, but the cat had vanished. Then they heard a scratching noise under the table.

"The beggar's at my scrap bucket!" cried Cook. "Quick, sling the sack over it and whack it one."

Twiggy did exactly as he was told. The creature in the bag struggled for a few moments - until Twiggy thumped it with a cooking pot. Then they returned to the deck in triumph, bearing aloft their prize.

When Pegg opened the sack to put in the cannon ball there was a flurry of feathers. The creature in the sack was King George.

For quite some moments Jethro Pegg was unable to speak as he stared at his dearly beloved parrot - who managed to squawk *"sharkbait"* very softly.

The ship's cook looked at Twiggy Blackstaff and Twiggy Blackstaff looked at the ship's cook.

"Oh no," groaned Cook.

"Not the plank, Cap'n, please not the plank," wailed Twiggy.

"Sharkbait!" said Pegg.

Chapter Six

Edmund Scurf was sorry to see the end of
Twiggy, for they had been planning to steal the
Captain's treasure together. Now it wouldn't be
so easy to sneak up on that miser Pegg and
surprise him. There was only himself on board
now - that pint-sized cabin boy didn't count.

However, that morning as he lay in his
hammock, Scurf came up with a beautiful plan.
First he went below and moved the gunpowder
into the treasure room. Then he moved the
treasure into the gunpowder room. When Pegg
came down to count his money, Scurf planned
to lock him in there and throw away the key.

He'd never get out. These rooms had walls like dungeons.

Scurf locked the gunpowder room from the inside. This would be a good place to listen for Pegg coming downstairs, and besides, he wanted to spend some time alone with the pile of wonderful silver and gold.

He held up a necklace to admire it by the light coming through a tiny, high window.

"It's all mine," he whispered in the deadly quiet. "I don't even have to share it with that fool Twiggy."

But suddenly there was a different kind of
light, and Scurf discovered to his horror that he
was not alone. The firetail cat was there.

"You!" cried Scurf.

A shower of sparks escaped from her coat
like a blaze of jumping fleas. And she had the
key in her mouth! She streaked up the wall to
escape through the high little window.

Without the key, Scurf knew that he was trapped. He was trapped with a hoard of silver and gold when what he needed most was just an ordinary old iron crowbar.

"You'd better do some serious thinking, Scurf," he thought. "Or you're sharkbait."

Chapter Seven

William worked hard all morning while Jethro Pegg scanned the horizon through a telescope.

"We'll have to find a port and get this ship fit to sail again," said Pegg. "And I need another crew. Where has that idle swine Scurf got to?"

"I haven't seen him, sir," said William.

"Bring me a candle, boy, it's time I counted my treasure. Then take the wheel of the ship and steer us north-west."

After fetching a candle, William took the wheel of the *Belinda* and held it steady.

He hadn't a clue where they were going in this empty ocean.

Miaow. He saw the firetail cat. She stood in a small dinghy at the back of the ship, motionless. Again she miaowed. William had the strangest feeling that the cat was talking to him.

Now she turned herself around before settling on a sack at the bottom of the dinghy. Was it only chance that she lay there on the very sack in which they had been prisoners together?

"What are you doing in the dinghy, Firetail?" he asked her.

She pointed at him with her tail, which then curled forward as if to motion him towards her. Or was that just his imagination? It occurred to him that there would never be a better chance to escape from this awful ship. *Come away with me now, Trevithick*, she seemed to say, *take your chance in this dinghy on the open sea.*

"All right then!" said William, loosening the ropes on the dinghy. "But I hope you know what you're doing, cat. Here goes."

The small boat splashed into the water below, and William rowed away from the *Belinda* as fast as he could.

At that moment Jethro Pegg, with a candle in his hand and King George upon his shoulder, had arrived at the bottom of the stairs.

Something creaked in the room labelled
GUNPOWDER, NO LIGHTS. Rats, most likely.
That blasted cat was a no-good dud.

Inside the treasure room he set down his
candle near some loose gunpowder (for Scurf
had been careless) and the gunpowder began to
sizzle. As it sizzled the gunpowder gave off
blue sparks which were not unlike a firetail cat
glowing in the dark.

Then came the BOOM.

Chapter Eight

William Trevithick could hardly believe his eyes. What had been the good ship *Belinda* simply didn't exist any more. A few planks floated here and there to mark where she went down, that was all.

"That is unbelievable!" he gasped, glancing suspiciously at the cat. "Did you have anything to do with that, Firetail?"

A fluttering creature wearing a few blackened feathers landed in the bow of the boat. It squawked for some time before calming down.

"You too!" said William. "Well, here we are - the ship's cat, the Captain's parrot and the cabin boy, all stuck in the middle of the ocean in a dinghy."

"Sharkbait!" screeched King George.

"That's exactly what I'm afraid of," agreed William. "Unless you have any bright ideas, Firetail?"

The firetail cat curled herself into a contented ball, for all the world as if she knew something that a mere cabin boy couldn't know.

Look out for more titles in the Storybooks series:

Dreamy Daniel, Brainy Bert by Scoular Anderson

Daniel is always getting into trouble at school. But with the help of the brainy class mouse, Bert, Daniel learns to beat his day-dreaming habit.

Look Out, Loch Ness Monster! by Keith Brumpton

For as long as he can remember, Kevin McAllister has longed to see the Loch Ness Monster. Then, one dark Scottish night, his dream comes true!

The Twenty Ton Chocolate Mountain by Helen Muir

Mr McWeedie doesn't teach the children much about reading or adding up. Instead, he tells them about spaghetti trees and singing sunflowers – and the Twenty Ton Chocolate Mountain.

Hurray for Monty Ray! by Sam McBratney

Monty Ray has a new baby brother – the sixth boy in the family! Nobody can think of a name for the new baby, so he's just called Lamb Chop. Monty Ray is very worried – what if the name sticks?

Nigel the Pirate by Roy Apps

When Cap'n Bonegrinder knocked on the door asking for apprentice boy pirates, Nigel thought this was his chance to make his mark on the world. But Nigel's hopes were soon sunk on board 'The Bloody Plunderer'.

Tall Tale Tom by Anne Forsyth

Tom is an ordinary black-and-white cat with an extraordinary talent for making up tall tales. His fibs always land him in trouble, until the day that he finds himself the hero of the whole town!

Storybooks can be bought from your local bookshop or can be ordered direct from the publishers. For more information, write to: *The Sales Department, Macdonald Young Books Ltd, Campus 400, Maylands Avenue, Hemel Hempstead HP2 7EZ.*